_____'s

Jungle Book

Published by Scholastic Inc., 90 Old Sherman Turnpike,
Danbury, Connecticut 06816.

For information regarding permission, write to:
Disney Licensed Publishing, 114 Fifth Avenue, New York, New York 10011.

0-7172-8336-4

Printed by Norhaven Book, Denmark

First printing, November 2006

Walt Disney's
THE JUNGLE BOOK

SCHOLASTIC INC.

New York Toronto London Auckland Sydney
Mexico City New Delhi Hong Kong Buenos Aires

Deep in the Indian jungle, Bagheera the panther heard a strange sound. He discovered that it was a Man-cub! The baby boy was in a basket, which lay in a half-sunken boat on the river.

Bagheera felt sorry for the baby. He carefully carried the basket ashore.

"The Man-cub will never survive without a mother," Bagheera said to himself. Then he remembered that a wolf family lived nearby. Perhaps they would adopt the Man-cub.

Bagheera brought the basket to the wolves'
den. When the mother wolf and her cubs found
the laughing baby, they smiled. Rama, the father
wolf, was not so pleased at first. But soon he, too,
was smiling at the Man-cub.

The wolves named the Man-cub "Mowgli." For ten years, he lived happily in the jungle.

Mowgli learned many things from the wolves: how to scratch himself . . .

. . . how to play dead . . .

. . . and how to run!

But one day, there was some terrible news in the jungle. Shere Khan the tiger had returned. The fearsome tiger hated all humans because a hunter had once shot at him. So Mowgli was in danger!

Late that night, the wolf pack gathered with Bagheera on Council Rock. They decided that Mowgli must leave. Bagheera knew of a Man-village, where he could take Mowgli and he would be safe.

But taking Mowgli to the Man-village
would not be easy.

"This is my home," protested Mowgli,
as Bagheera tried to pry him from a tree.
"I don't want to leave the jungle!"

Reluctantly, Mowgli
began the journey to the
Man-village with Bagheera.

Night began to fall. When they came to a big
tree, Bagheera decided they would spend the night
there. Bagheera gave the boy a lift up.

"Go to sleep," Bagheera told Mowgli, as they
settled themselves on a branch.

But they were not alone. Kaa the snake was hiding in the tree. He thought Mowgli would make a tasty treat!

"Yes, Man-cub," Kaa whispered, as he slithered down the tree, "go to sssleep."

Mowgli woke up and saw Kaa. "Leave me alone," he said to the snake.

"Do not be afraid, Man-cub," said Kaa. "Trussst me. Go to sssleep."

Kaa stared at Mowgli. Mowgli began to feel dizzy. He was under Kaa's spell. Kaa wrapped his long tail around Mowgli.

Just then Bagheera
woke up. He slapped
Kaa with his paw before
the snake could hurt
Mowgli. Kaa fell to the
ground with a THUD!

"You have made a ssserious missstake, Bagheera," said Kaa, as he slithered off.

Bagheera told Mowgli, "You see, the jungle is too dangerous for you. You belong in the Man-village. We will go there in the morning."

But Mowgli still did not want to live in the
Man-village. So he left early the next morning.
"I can take care of myself!" Mowgli said to
Bagheera, as he walked away. "I don't need anyone."
But after a while, Mowgli felt very lonely.

Then Mowgli heard somebody singing.
It was Baloo—a big, friendly bear.
"Well, hello there, Little Britches," Baloo
said to Mowgli, with a smile.
They quickly became friends.

Baloo taught
Mowgli how to
dance like a bear . . .

. . . and growl like a bear . . .

. . . and even how to fight like a bear!

"I want to stay in the jungle with you, Baloo!" said Mowgli.

23

"I like being a bear," Mowgli told Baloo, as they floated down the river.

Neither of them noticed that several monkeys were watching them.

Before Baloo could stop
them, the monkeys grabbed
Mowgli! They brought Mowgli
to their leader, King Louie.

"So you're the
Man-cub," said King
Louie. "Crazy!"
"I'm not crazy.
You are!" said Mowgli.

"Have some bananas," said King Louie, shoving two into Mowgli's mouth. King Louie struck a deal so that Mowgli could stay in the jungle. Then the monkeys decided to celebrate. Everybody started dancing.

Meanwhile, Baloo found the ancient ruins where
the monkeys lived. In order to rescue Mowgli, Baloo
disguised himself as a big monkey and danced right
into the party.

Baloo's plan worked! While the monkeys sang
and danced, he carried Mowgli out of the ruins.

"Thanks for rescuing me," said Mowgli. "I didn't want to be a monkey. I would rather be a bear, like you."

"But you are not a bear," Baloo said sadly. "The jungle is too dangerous for you. You belong in the Man-village."

"You are just like Bagheera!" shouted Mowgli. "I don't want to go to the Man-village! I can take care of myself!"

So Mowgli ran away from Baloo, too.

Mowgli ran through the jungle.
Then he ran right into Shere Khan!

"Do you know who I am, Man-cub?"
asked Shere Khan.

"Yes. But I am not afraid of you,"
said Mowgli.

"Everyone is afraid of me," Shere Khan said smugly.

"Well you don't scare me," said Mowgli.

"Ah, you have spirit for one so small," said the tiger.
"You deserve a sporting chance. I will close my eyes and
count to ten. It makes the chase more interesting."

Shere Khan began to count. But Mowgli didn't run
away. He wasn't about to be bullied by the tiger.

This only angered Shere Khan. Just as
he lunged for Mowgli, Baloo came to the
rescue! He grabbed the tiger's tail to try
to save the Man-cub.

Suddenly a bolt of lightning flashed in the sky. The lightning hit a nearby tree, starting a fire.

Mowgli picked up a burning branch and tied it to Shere Khan's tail. There was only one thing Shere Khan feared:

FIRE.

He let out a roar and fled.

Bagheera and
Baloo were so happy
to see that Mowgli
was not hurt!

"We're glad you're safe, Little Britches," said Baloo, when Mowgli ran up to the big bear and gave him a big hug.

Mowgli hugged Bagheera, too. He was happy to see his friends.

It was beginning to get dark,
so they found a safe place to rest.
Soon they were all fast asleep.

The following morning,
the three friends walked to the
river. Mowgli was explaining to
Baloo and Bagheera how
he could stay in the
jungle—especially
now that Shere
Khan had
gone away.

When they arrived at the river, they heard someone
singing. They crept closer and saw a young girl fetching
some water from the river.

"What's that?" asked Mowgli.

"Forget about those," said Baloo. "They're nothing
but trouble."

Mowgli decided to take a closer look. The girl turned and saw him. She smiled at Mowgli and dropped her jug of water.

"Hey, she did that on purpose!" Baloo said, watching from the bushes.

"Quite right," said the wise panther, with a smile.

Mowgli quickly picked up the jug the young girl had dropped and refilled it with water. Then he waved good-bye to his friends and followed her into the Man-village.

"Well, Baloo, Mowgli will live in the Man-village from now on," said Bagheera, as they headed back into the jungle. "We will miss him, but he is where he belongs."

"Yes," agreed Baloo, "but I still think he would have made one swell bear!"

The End

Here's some jungle fun!

Look back in the story and try to find these wild pictures.